TO HATTIE, TILLY, AND JASPER
RICK AND LAVONA
AND SARAH —R.M.

TO MY CHILDHOOD LEFTOVERS,
WHICH I WOULD HAPPILY DEVOUR NOW —H.A.

STERLING CHILDREN'S BOOKS
New York

An Imprint of Sterling Publishing Co., Inc.
1166 Avenue of the Americas
New York, NY 10036

Text © 2018 Ryan Miller
Cover and interior illustrations © 2018 Hatem Aly

ISBN 978-1-4549-2562-0

Distributed in Canada by Sterling Publishing Co., Inc.
C/o Canadian Manda Group, 664 Annette Street
Toronto, Ontario M6S 2C8, Canada
Distributed in the United Kingdom by GMC Distribution Services
Castle Place, 166 High Street, Lewes, East Sussex BN7 1XU, England
Distributed in Australia by NewSouth Books, 45 Beach Street, Coogee, NSW 2034, Australia

For information about custom editions, special sales, and premium
and corporate purchases, please contact Sterling Special Sales
at 800-805-5489 or specialsales@sterlingpublishing.com.

Manufactured in China

Lot #:
2 4 6 8 10 9 7 5 3 1
05/18

sterlingpublishing.com

Cover and interior design by Heather Kelly

HOW TO
FEED YOUR
PARENTS

by
RYAN MILLER

illustrated by
HATEM ALY

STERLING CHILDREN'S BOOKS
New York

Matilda Macaroni wanted to try quiche.

Her parents did not.

The list of things Mr. and Mrs. Macaroni would eat was very short.

CHICKEN

(only in nugget form, with barbecue sauce)

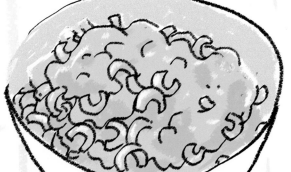

ELBOW MACARONI

(only mixed with orange-colored powder from a packet)

BURGERS

(only from a bag with ketchup, fries, and a toy)

GRILLED CHEESE

(only on white bread, cut into triangles)

PIZZA

(only topped with pepperoni
and delivered to their door)

CEREAL

(only if it was sugary and turned
the milk a different color)

They refused to even try anything else.

Matilda first discovered she liked other foods when
Grandma Macaroni brought over a pot of jambalaya
for a surprise treat one evening.

"YUCK!"
Matilda's dad said
when he saw the pot.

"NO WAY!"
Matilda's mom
said when she
smelled the steam.

They pushed their plates to the center of the table and sulked.

But Matilda was curious.

The jambalaya was interesting. It was surprising. It was . . .

DELICIOUS!

After that, Matilda tried new foods whenever she could. She got gumbo and goulash at Grandma's, sampled some sushi at a sleepover, and polished off a plate of pork paprikash on a play date.

But she soon realized that if she ever wanted to eat more than nuggets and noodles at home, she would have to commandeer the kitchen and cook for herself.

She started by learning how to crack eggs.

First she didn't tap them hard enough to break the shell.

Then she tapped them a little *too* hard.

Finally, she got it just right.

She worked with her grandma to learn oven safety and knife safety and all of the other safeties she could think of. She started reading cookbooks as bedtime stories.

She gave her allowance to her babysitter to buy ingredients from the local farmers' market.

Matilda practiced with a willing grown-up whenever she could. Soon, she had perfected paella, mastered miso soup, and conquered croquettes.

She wanted to share every dish with her parents. She knew they would enjoy them if they would only try them. So she came up with a plan.

"I'll handle dinner tonight," she said one morning at breakfast.

"NO QUICHE!"
her mom said.

"NOTHING FUNNY!"

her dad added.

"Burgers," Matilda said.
"Just burgers."

Her parents were both
running late, so they
slurped the bright purple
milk from the bottom of
their bowls and agreed.

That night, Matilda's parents stared
skeptically at the food in front of them.

"This doesn't look like what I like," her dad whined.

"It's a hamburger," Matilda said innocently.

"I'm going to warm up some leftovers," her mom said.

"The fridge is empty!" her dad yelped. "No pizza! No nuggets!"

"This is what's for dinner," Matilda said. "If you're hungry, you can eat. If you're not, don't. But I made this, and this is what we're having."

"You made this?" Mrs. Macaroni asked. She lifted the bun and peered at the patty. "There are mushrooms on it. And green things."

"That's arugula," Matilda said. "You're going to love it."

Mrs. Macaroni raised one eyebrow, but then her stomach growled. Loudly.

"Our daughter *made* this," she said to her husband. She took the teeniest, tiniest bite.

"It's interesting," she said, chewing slowly. "It's surprising. It's . . .

DELICIOUS!"

Mr. Macaroni smiled politely at Matilda and took a teeny, tiny bite of his own.

"Hey—this isn't bad," he said. "Actually, it's good!"

"I can make it again," Matilda said as her parents chowed down. "But I was thinking that maybe I could try to bake a quiche first."

"I don't think you should do any more cooking," her dad replied. "I think *we* should do it together."

"We can take turns picking recipes," her mom said. "We might not like everything—"

"But we promise to try anything," her dad finished.

The next night, Matilda and her parents sprinkled some flour on the counter. They rolled out dough before filling it with eggs, spinach, bacon, Swiss cheese, and more. The quiche was a hit. As was just about everything they made.

"FANTASTIC FAJITAS!" her dad said after he bit into a warm, handmade tortilla stuffed with steak, colorful peppers, and onions.

"EXCELLENT EGGPLANT PARMESAN!" her mom said while going back for a second slice of the purple vegetable with oregano-spiced sauce and mozzarella cheese.

"PHENOMENAL PHO!" they both said as they leaned over their bowls and slurped up rice noodles floating in ginger-scented beef broth.

"You know," Matilda's mom said, talking around a mouthful of garlic naan and chicken tikka masala, "I think I might like to try some jambalaya."

They called up Grandma and asked her to bring over her signature dish.

"Amazing!" Grandma exclaimed when she saw that Mr. and Mrs. Macaroni started eating with no complaints. "Matilda, you've done a great job of getting them to try new foods!"

"Thank you," Matilda said. "Now if only I
could get them to keep their room clean."

THE
MACARONI
FAMILY QUICHE RECIPE

Make your own quiche, just like Matilda and her parents!
Ask an adult for help using tools like sharp knives or the
oven. This recipe makes two quiches, so you can eat
one right away and freeze the other for later.

QUICHE CRUST

INGREDIENTS

- 2 cups flour
- 1 teaspoon salt
- 3 tablespoons olive oil

- 2/3 cup butter
- 6 tablespoons ice water
  (can use up to 8 if needed)

DIRECTIONS

1) Pre-heat oven to 350° F.

2) In a large bowl, mix all ingredients by hand or with a pastry
   blender into a firm dough.

2) With floured hands, separate dough into two equal-sized balls.

3) On a floured work surface, roll out one floured ball with a rolling
   pin, turning it a quarter turn clockwise every three rolls until
   you have a circle 12 inches in diameter. Always roll away from
   your body.

4) Carefully press the circle of dough into a 9-inch pie dish, using
   any overhang to create a slightly thicker rim of crust. Poke bottom
   of crust with a fork in several places to prevent bubbling.

5) Repeat steps 3 and 4 with the other ball of dough.

6) Bake each for 10 minutes (they won't be fully cooked) before
   adding filling.